Other books by Randy Thornhorn:

THE KESTREL WATERS
A Tale Of Love And Devil
(sequel to *Wicked Temper*)

WICKED TEMPER
A Riddle Top Novel

HOWLS OF A HELLHOUND ELECTRIC
Riddle Top Magpies & Bobnot Boogies

Visit Randy Thornhorn online at

www.thornhorn.com

Rosasharn Press
244 Fifth Avenue
Suite C-118
New York, N.Y. 10001
www.rosasharnpress.com

ISBN 978-0-9916496-6-2

Printed in the United States of America.

Limited Edition

for Pegatha

THE AXMAN'S SHIFT

by

Randy Thornhorn

The new clock rocked and went chinga-linga-linga.

Lady Floy flopped and rocked the bed. The canopy ballooned, straining the four-poster. Floy's swollen lips sucked in the chinga-linga-linga then blew some ching back out with a bit of a whistle. The whistle came out the hole where one dog tooth used to be. Her other dog tooth was doing just fine, thanks for asking. The new clock kept rocking as Floy puckered and flopped, trying to wake up.

Floy was big. Floy had always been a big bed rocker. And her bouffant heart was even bigger than her canopy bed. This meant Floy's bed and heart were full of love, love overflowing, meaning both were too big for her teensy, dark bedroom. Most axmen could barely squeeze in, if they even wanted to squeeze in. And, even then, they could only squeeze in around Floy's bulging edges.

Chinga-linga-linga.

Waking up at 3:00 a.m. was never easy. That's why Floy always left an alarm clock cranked, set, and waiting to rock on the cedar chest. This precaution forced Floy to climb off the foot of the bed to shush the damn chinga-ling. This kept her from shushing it then falling back asleep. Tonight was no different. Waking up at 3:00 a.m. for her ax-killer was never going to be easy. But she had to prove her love.

Tonight was no different. Chinga-linga-ling-ling.

Once again, Lady Floy began to surface. She sneezed twice, still clinging to the remnant of a dream. A dream about a creepy woman—a Lych woman—at Floy's kitchen window. In her dream the Lych woman's face was melting, but the creepy hag seemed okay with that. The Lych woman shined a shimmering mirror through the kitchen glass so Lady Floy could see herself. Floy looked into the mirror, admiring her own tomato-red cheekbones and movie star smile.

"How went your tizzypoke?" the Lych woman asked. "How many magpie fit the tree? How went your ax-baby?" she say.

Lady Floy did not reply. Because, before she could answer that weird woman, Floy's sugar plums and plump rumpkin were chinga-linged awake, yearning for her axman's return. Because Floy kept setting the clock. On the cedar chest. Off the foot of the bed. So she could be here with big open arms, ready for his nocturnal homecomings.

Chinga-linga-linga.

The alarm finally made Floy crawl to the foot of bed, so she could look at the clock and stop it. She hit the floor, crushing the clock—(*chinga-blunk*) — and wondering how soon she could get the icebox fixed. That icebox had been broken for over two weeks. Glancing out her real and undreamt kitchen window, Lady saw no Lych woman now. She only saw velvet blackness with the first falling flecks of snow.

Floy drank a warm NuGrape while she waited on the divan. She spread her huge body lengthwise on the cushions like a centerfold filling out a chiffon circus tent, her pudgy toes gripping the padded arm of the divan. The hula lamp gave purple glow to her bosom. Looking at the lamp, she noticed her axman's Big Chief tablet lying on the side table under the hula girl's grass skirt. Floy picked up the tablet, flipping it open.

The page Floy landed on had plenty of his habitual pencil scratchings. Along the edges were all manner of odds-and-end doodles. At the top he had written "E" and "A minor" and "F#" (F Sharp), then he had crossed out the "F#"—replacing it with "D7".

Below the D7 were some of his scribbled lyrics:

Baby its a crime you aint never been kissed
we all lose our heds on the axmans shift

This made Floy smile and sigh, with a bit of whistle out her dogtooth hole. Her ax-daddy could chop up a jump tune anytime the spirit moved him. Oh, yes, he had the chops. By the time his chops stopped chopping, that crowd was pie-eyed and fried. Why, it was enough to make Floy hungry. His chops were but one of many reasons to love him. And wasn't love just another pang of hunger?

Lady Floy flipped a few more pages before her eyes fell on more words in a tighter, more unsteady hand:

I been climbing in houses at night
* where I listen to women*
who shudder
*   with prickly heat*
Along that tremr of sleep
* they whimper now an nuzzle up*
to a phantm heartbeat
* a cut and bleeding fever king*
Who seethes and sighs
* in every verging*
* stairwell dark*
harkning from the depth
of her rising breast
*   from the deep below*

* I been climbing in houses at night*
*   where I listen to women*
to wanting women
* Who never want to know.*

These did not seem like song lyrics to Lady Floy—not like any lyric she had ever heard him sing. She would have to discuss these words with him, for better understanding and clarification.

———

At 3:36 she heard his motorcycle. She heard his feet scuffing outside. He was juiced and loose, like always. He only dragged his feet when he was juiced. Always the same refrain. He came in the door, tracking snow on her rug. He leaned his Gibson guitar beside the electric outlet, beneath the purple glow of hula lamp, like he might jump start his axe later with some raw voltage and no damn amp.

"Lovell?" she said, sitting upright.

"Hullo baby," he drawled, veering sidelong toward the kitchen.

Floy wished Lovell would put on some more meat. His glittery gold palomino vest hung slack around his ribcage. The devilish beard did little to hide his ruin.

"Where you going, doll?" she asked, standing barefoot.

"Samwich..."

"Wait, I'll make you a sandwich. But talk to me, talk to this baby first."

He rotated on his boot heel, bleary-eyed, unsteady in the kitchen door. She beckoned with a thick purplish finger.

"C'mere..." she whispered.

He was wary, and weak. His screwed-up eyes goggled from corner to corner of the dim parlor, then back to her. He scuffed over and she folded her arms around his scrawny hips. Smothered in the folds of her teats and belly, he coughed a ragged cough that reeked smoke and gin.

Floy's lips swelled out to kiss and nibble his ear-lobe. "Did you sang good? Did they go fer you doll?"

He closed his eyes and tried not to puke. He loved her. How could he tell her he was sick but still loved her?

"Ummm-hmmm, sure, sang gooood," he fumbled, "sang damn good, hehheh."

"And they loved you up, didn't they doll?"

"Afffer while. Afffer while they'uzzz hootin real damn good."

"I'm so proud of you."

"Thank ye, hon. I'm proud yeeew tooo."

She tongued his ear canal. "So let's count the boodle," she whispered.

"Awww, the *booodle...*"

Floy's head reared back, her eyes searching for his, trying to catch his restless gaze.

" Give moomoo her coozy cash." She was firm, clamping him into her bosom.

"Dammmmn, woman, I fergits to tell ye. Din't git no boodle tonight. Mr. Bull was short on his till, couldn't pay me right off. Pay me nexxx weeeek..." He wriggled a little, wanting his onion and toma-to sandwich.

Floy did not let go.

"You're a-lying to me now, ain't you? So's you can spend it on more dranks and other nookies, ain't you? Just tell me where it's hid this time and I'll fix you a bite to eat."

He shook his long face with fervor. "Mr. Bull din't pay...pay nexxx week."

Floy released her grip and the axman sank away as she *walloped* him upside his ear with a glancing blow. Lovell fell towards the floor but she caught him then threw his lank body across the room.

The hula lamp exploded.

She waddled over, grabbing him by the scruff, pitching him hard into the front door. A new crack split in the door panel as he bled and slumped forward, mumbling something useless.

"Where's my honey money, you needledink?" she spat like the adder.

He gave no answer. No, not yet.

She flipped him over hard, like a splat of Vidalia onion, sweet and scorching on her griddle. Why did her axman always make her take big bites? She hated to take big bites, just to prove her love. But one way or the other, Lovell Starling would cough up all her gold and green. He would cough it all up if it took Floy all this livelong night.

So Floy doused him with warm NuGrape. Then she leapt, bellyflopping on his golden palomino.

Mercy.

The big guitar almost fell from his arms, but his

left hand saved it.

"Lovell Starling, hold your headbone still!"

It hurt when Dora Hannah barked in his aching ear as she tried to dab him with iodine. His ear had been bleeding slow for three days. It stung like a bitch when she dabbed him—and besides—Lovell seldom sat still when sober. And right now he was sober. Sick and sober. But not for long.

Dora began to gently poke cotton into his ear hole. Sheriff Bull Hannah lumbered into his own office in back of Bull's Gladiola Lounge and laid his mandolin on the desk in front of Lovell.

"You welcome to sleep the night here, Lovell," Bull grinned, watching his star attraction suffer. "If you've a mind to. Or if you've a mind at all."

His wife Dora tee-heed, packing away her first aid kit. Lovell Starling was still stinging, flinching.

"I'm diggin' yer drift," Lovell said from the Sheriff's desk chair. "Them roads be too iced over for no bike to bop."

"I copy that," Bull nodded. "In fact, I am way ahead of you, son. I rolled your motor-sickle out the parkin' lot and parked it up under the swamp coolers against the building, out of the element."

"That's why he's High Sheriff, folks," Lovell mused, tenderly touching his sore ear. "Thank ya, Bull."

"You oughta get ye a doctor to look at that," Dora advised. "Don't be foolin' round when it comes to yer ears, mister. Good Lord only give us two to hearken with. Won't be handin' out no more in this life."

She shook her head as Lovell grunted. She knew he was not going to pay what little money Floy left him to any doctors.

"You tell that Floy that Dora Hannah says she needs to go easy on the cash cow."

Lovell grunted at that also, attempting a smile. The smile hurt because his jaw kept popping. He did not want to think about Floy right now. Lovell had made a pretty hot night of it, despite his throbbing ear, and he just wanted to get stoned. This was not wise, he knew. But Lovell Starling had always been smarter than wise.

Jack Rich—the new drummer for the The Posse Men—stuck his head in the office to wave goodnight. Jack was the last of the band to leave, it took him longer to break down his trap set and load it in his station wagon.

"What a night, Starboy," smiling Jack told him, "You killed a few ladies, didn't you?"

That was a given, everybody knew that. Jack left, with Dora and Bull Hannah close behind him.

Lovell waved bye-bye to them all.

"I'll lock that front door—" Lovell shouted out, slumped in the swivel chair.

"I copy that—" Bull bellowed from out in the dance hall, his mighty voice echoing through the deep empty building.

It had been a long night, it had been a short

night, Lovell was thinking. Was it only a half dozen hours ago that he had leapt onto that bandstand out there to face a house full of rawboned hillbillies?

Lovell Starling plugged his amp, slung his rhinestone-braid guitar strap and shot straight into *Axman's Shift*.

CHICKA-CHICKA-*TWAAAAAAAANG!*

It was quite a shock. Fisticuffs broke out stage left and the Big Fryday Beer Brawl was *on*. Lovell bent strings till they were white-hot, chasing demons with his big guitar until the whole roadhouse woke up screaming, help me mama, screaming for more. He sang like a nighthawk soaring, then swooping for the kill. Baptismal juices flowed, salty lather soon dripping from his long pointed sideburns and devilish Van Dyke beard, evil and black, goddamn the grey. Lovell booted a bloody trucker off the bandstand as his third gut-torn, staccato guitar break ripped loose, took over.

> *Whaaaaay-yell,*
> *We all lose our heads*
> *on the Axman's shift—*

Hell, he might be getting old, but his axe never aged a day. A dental plate ricocheted off the mike-stand. Call the doctor.

"*Hook it, daddy, hook it!*" they pled.

"*Mercy—*" he cried, spiraling down his frets.

Smoke swirled, glittering swirls in velvet black ether. Out the corner of his eye, Lovell saw the Bull's bar mallet strike paydirt, a body dropped, ending the stage-side ruckus just as Lovell skidded through the last bars of *Axman's Shift*. The applause never let up. Lovell gave no second chances before kicking out all stops on *Wreckin' Ball Blues*, another hell-bent boogie of his own:

Work me, work me,
   I ride a wreckin' ball!

So they worked him and Lovell worked them. Up one side and down the other.

All day, all night, baby,
   Your trainman hear the call!
   (Ride that wreckin' ball—)

When he *how-wow-wowled* like a night train his jaw would pop. Bad. Christ, would that snap in his jaw never heal? Blood crackled in his left ear. But the crowd didn't hear it. They heard the chugalug, the boomlayboom, the squall in his left-hand digits, the gunshot in his picker—the godawful beat and the glory. They rode that wrecking ball around the horn and back, stamping their feet, begging for release. But that wild-eyed, jumping-blues engineer danced across the stage and who would not let go.

The Posse Men, Bull Hannah's house band—raised on bluegrass—did their best to keep up.

Sure, Lovell gave his crew the wink during a neck-choking lick. The boys did all right. For bluegrass pickers. Tip Lee's doghouse bass thumped up a storm and Lovell loved him some Jack Rush drums. It felt good to finally have a drummer. Jack Rush could have held down the beat in any New Orleans stomp joint.

A lot the common folk had come for mountain dirges and backholler tunes—and looked surprised to get wildman Lovell Starling instead. It was a late booking. Bull Hannah knew Lovell needed the bread, and Bull was always good for a last minute gig, fast money. And damned if the common man didn't take to his Starling shenanigans like dirty ducks to water. Didn't they just always? After *Wrecking Ball* he made another shift, and sank into *Sic Em Dogs On Down*, a raunchy slow-burn rip-off he'd reheated from Amos Milburn's *One Scotch, One Bourbon, One Beer*. Lovell didn't worry it. Most of this bunch had never heard of Amos Milburn, and Lovell stole to survive.

A little later, Bull himself came up for a couple of his trademark mandolin jigs. One of the Posse Men, a beau named Dexter, stepped forward to strum rhythm guitar and harmonize on *Going Up Caney*. Bull sang tenor. Lovell helped out with a cushion of jazz chords. It worked, didn't it?

He watched them cheer, those hardscrabble faces, roaring, clapping calluses. After twenty years of this, he saw them clap and roar in his sleep. Mud pounders in their one good shirt, pomade hair slicker than an Arab's heel. Young buck-rutting sharpies fresh and damp out of the patch, making payments on bad, barren dirt, a Ford, a kid or three. And the women. There was always the women. Painted, waxed and plenty willing. His people. They cheered Bull off the stage. That giant, fearless, god-fearing rascal loved every last squeal as he hung his mandolin back over the bar where it swung nightly from the boar's snout.

By that time—*POW-CHICKKKA-POW-POW—TWAAAAAANG!*—Lovell was rocking the joint again with *Backdoor To Glory.*

"*Go, baby, goooo!*" the gals hollered, shaking their hips.

"*Go, man, goooo!*" their menfolk railed.

"*Cut em up!*" Tip Lee winked from in back of his upright bass.

Inside Bull's Gladiola Lounge it was a killing floor. You could go to Jesus but first you had hell to pay. All told, Lovell played for six hours. Ending his last number with a crashing chord, his face dripping, Lovell looked down and saw that no-good devil had busted his D-string.

Shortly after two a.m., when Lovell finally flipped off his amp, the house was mostly dizzy, vacu-

um-packed, withered flesh. One by one, they bad-
gered and filed out that door, wanting more, talking
trash, giving Bull Hannah the high sign as they
headed home through the snow, trudging back to
their cold, cold lives.

Two hours later, the roadhouse was dark, getting more arctic by the minute, as Lovell camped
alongside the woodstove in Bull's back office. He
was stoned and alone. His favorite disposition. The
only proper dessert for his delectable Mars bar supper. The only bad thing about not going home tonight was the limited dining fare after hours here
at the Gladiola. Lovell would have preferred to doctor some slum-gullion in a skillet loaded with onion,
sage, and black pepper. Floy even had two leftover
cathead biscuits in a bowl in the icebox, if she hadn't
devoured them yet. In his mind's eye, Lovell could
see those catheads soaking up pot liquor alongside
his slum-gullion right about now. Two things he
could damn well do: Lovell knew how to outpick and
outcook any cash cowboy in the rodeo.

Outside, yesterday's snowstorm revived itself,
swelling to blizzard proportions. The wind clattered,
straining tin and tarpaper, riffing a nasty snare on
the attic fan. If this kept up those roads would soon
be nothing but glass and snowdrifts. Tomorrow
night at Bull's looked to be a bust.

Lovell sat on the floor, wrapped in a throw rug,
rolling more laughing tobacco in brown paper. His

fingers were slow but sure. He had already popped the little pink pill. The beer made Lovell's eardrum swell, his jawbone ached after a night's singing, but no matter goddammit. He would not go home. She was home waiting for him and he would not oblige. Fuck her. She should never have walloped his ear.

Floy.

Floy, Fla-Floy, Floy.

Fuck her.

Fortunately for Lovell, good old Bull Hannah didn't mind his favorite picker parking overnight at the club. Dig that. Why, Lovell even had his own key. Hadn't he been busting his hump long enough at this racket to rate a few keys of his own? Couldn't anybody, *any-body* see that? Couldn't *she* by-Jesus see that much? Well, his Indian Scout motorcycle sat outside in the freeze. And Floy had thrown a rod on the Buick, so she couldn't even come looking for him. Thank the Lord for itty-bitty favors and pass the fucking churchkey.

Lovell fumbled and found his churchkey, pierced another can of Jax. It was good to be drunk. Knee-walking, goggle-eyed, dick-dragging drunk. Christ if he couldn't still knee-walk his way to the mike and play another six mother-humping hours without slipping a beat. If he only had a D-string.

If he only had a D-string he could still lay them flat till daybreak. But what was the percentage in that? Did he even care anymore?

It was supposed to be different by now. He was supposed to have the mansion on high and the gold-dipped Lincoln with a Continental kit, the record deals and the Hollywood contracts. Lovell took stock of the jammed office. Broom. Desk. Ledgers. Spittoon. His *f*-holed Gibson Super 400 axe lay atop cardboard crates of soda straws and napkins. After twenty-plus years of trying to peddle his white stripe of goosed-up, electrified country boy blues, he was about tuckered out. He had already dragged Floy through every tinpot juke and beer hall in the Mid-South before returning home, busted. She was his bag to drag. All those years had told him one thing. These dirt-eaters might go for his high-voltage shenanigans. Bull Hannah might even hire him weekends. But the big record men in the big cities were not buying. Lately, another rumor teased Lovell as so many had taunted him before. He had heard tell of some stud kid burning up the local radio down in Natchez or Memphis somewhere, some mercury-throated white boy stomping the blues. They said this crazy dee-jay had made a record on him and was looking for even more boogaloo kings.

Lovell had heard such cat-teasings before. If he were a younger man, if it had not been so many decades since he first carved a slot in his guitar then screwed that P90 cobalt-mag pickup into the maple sunburst, if he were not routinely smarter than wise—why, Lovell might just run that silly ass rumor down. And if he did so, one more time, as sure as this snow on his roof, he would draw the joker like he always had done. It was good to be drunk. No radio receptions intruded this far. *If* be fucking damned. Nashville wanted the jug and fiddle stuff while New York wanted horns and strings. And Lovell wanted another Jax. He opened his fifth and lay scribbling snatches of lyric on a manila envelope. After a while, his pencil drew werewolves and goblins along the edge.

He would have to go home in the morning, so the twins of dawn and dread clung together in his brain pan. She would try to beat hell out of him if he didn't fork over tonight's pay. When Lovell was sober, she didn't stand a chance. But he was weary. Weary of the dirt-eaters and the beaver-go-round, weary of chasing his tail, and goddam it, he was tired of her. Floy. And being tired of Floy made him wonder sometimes if he wasn't sour on his guitar too. What had the axe ever gotten him really, except a scrapbook of failures, some forgotten poontang, and endless nights of super-charged euphoria that hooked him like Sister Morphine. He came back night after night, pick in hand, needing the thrill, the electric jism. Often his fingers bled on stage, he needed it so bad.

Other than this nightly jolt, Lovell had nothing or next to it. Floy had kin hereabouts. Lovell's clan had died out. Oh, he owned his axe and rhinestone glitter strap outright, his motorbike, a gold palomino vest, a pair of pointy, heel-worn Italian boots—and there was six acres of wet Alabama real estate he had never seen, willed by his nasty Great Grandma Zee, may she rest or die trying. A son-of-a-bitch-born-Satan, that's what she called Lovell Starling for playing devil's music. Grammy Zee once smashed all his demo records in a crutch-swinging rage. And, recently, her run-amok great-grandbaby Lovell was glad she had done it. When you were flat-ass nowhere you did not need 78 revolutions going nowhere to remind you. Mirrors were reminder enough.

Yes friends, the drunkard told himself, Lovell Starling was tuckered out. He was pissing red and had quit plucking his silver hairs. Floy wanted to dye his lovey locks, but he wouldn't sit still for her. Dye your own rat's nest, bitch, not mine. That's what he told her. There were nights like these that Lovell just needed to kill something, anything. Somebody.

As he dozed off behind the stove, Lovell wondered what possible edge he could gain by hiding the bitter truth through hair dyes or any other lies to his ego. He had to yawn and face the music. The Axman's glory days were done. He might be getting tougher every day. But he was also getting older by the minute. Too damn old. The poet in Lovell Starling knew the only cure for such terminal cases was to bury the body in a dream. But the beer and reefer in Lovell Starling meant when drunk he never dreamt.

He just crashed like a common drunk driver.

The next morning, Saturday morning, was bitter cold, hushed and bright with glorification. Lovell let himself out of the club. He was so wasted, it didn't faze him much when he realized the frosty Indian's battery was dead. His bones hurt as he shuffled glumly toward Ewe Springs on foot, guitar strapped across his chest. He would have to reckon with Floy. A third of his pay was in his shoe, with a third stashed back at Bull's in the boar's gullet. He took an old, seldom-used shortcut through the remains of J.C. Dixon's snowbound, once-thriving lumber camp, then began walking upcountry along Six Bucket Run.

Hungover and ailing like a son-of-a-bitch-born-Satan, Lovell was whistling a rag nonetheless when the long, green Reo swept around the bend.

Over three hundred pounds of Floy Starling sat in the icy, unsealed privy. She was tugging on her rottenest tooth. It was tricky business. Floy wore her flounciest ritzy dress and did not want bloodstains around her cleavage, or worse—for her hem to snag in the pothole. This was her favorite dress of the scores in her boudoir. And, surprise, surprise, Lovell refused to pop for it, the cheap turd. She had to coldcock him when he came in drunk after the show. Floy wished he would quit making her roll him for the dough. But this little cocktail dress was worth every dollar-a-day Miss Doobelle spent stitching it. She knew gals who would sell their kids for such a dress. Champagne satin with a taffeta bodice.

Floy loved dainty things, her perty-perties, things of florid beauty like herself. She had to work at beauty of course, since under the rouge, the double eyelashes and thick black burgundy lipstick she was the most hatchet-faced girl to ever strut through Ewe Springs on stiletto heels. "A girl at heart, the soul of a lady," she always said.

She squirmed on the pothole. Stress gave her cramps. Frigid shithouses made her varicose veins throb. Ladyship was a bitch. Her bloody fingers probed the back of her mouth where a molar was tearing loose. What was another tooth or two at this stage? Why, Floy was seriously considering a charm bracelet designed to incorporate her oral extractions. Floy's make-up case held plenty of her uprooted fangs, each suitable for mounting. Naturally, this would mean getting Lovell to negotiate a ride down to Roanoke, to the jeweler. That might be trickier still. It was Wednesday and Lovell was five days missing.

The word was out, but so were Floy's snoop

hounds. Her homely nieces, Myrna and Kate, had driven back up to the house this morning on their diesel tractor. A good tractor was about all that could climb that snow-packed hill in this weather. Floy was just polishing off breakfast—six fried eggs and a pound of chicken livers—when she heard her boxy nieces jump onto the porch.

"Mawnin', Aintie Floy," Kate said, coming through the door.

"Mawnin', Aintie," Myrna shivered in behind her sister.

Floy gulped her last greasy liver, smacking a hello at them.

"Uncle Love show his face yit?" asked coal-thatched Kate, brushing snow off her overalls.

Floy yawned, picking her teeth with the glossy spike of her pinkie-nail. "Nope. The sumbitch is out gittin' liquored up on my money. You gals ask fer him at Bull Hannah's?"

"Yes'm, we asked." Kate scrunched her nose, frustrated. She was the oldest and had been through this too many times. "Bull says he'll keep his finger in the wind and not to worry, that tomcat will drag his guitar home soon as he's uncrossed his eyeballs."

"Crossed or uncrossed, it ain't his eyeballs Lady wants clipped. It ain't his eyeballs she wants dangling from her charm bracelet. It's Friday night's boodle bucks he's out there chuggin' while I sit here in the lap of misery. Our lifestyle teeters on the brink."

Myrna dropped into the chair opposite Floy. "Ain-tie Floy? Why don't ye jist accompany Uncle when he entertains the folks? Then you kin keep track of finances up front."

"Sure 'nough," Kate growled from the window, pouring coffee. "Snatch that boodle from ole Bull before Uncle Love kin."

Kate would not care one way or the other if it didn't put her out so much. She was more interested in the spotted fawn and mother doe crossing Floy's backyard.

Floy chuckled, showing a few spotty teeth. She lifted two mighty butt cheeks from her two creaking chairs.

"Look girlies, I spent more nights in more jiveboxes with that cheat than his own pecker did. I was still a size twenty when he kept reloading my Shirley Temple that New Year's Eve in Plowboy's beer joint, down to Roanoke. Eighteen hellacious years ago, gals." Floy pumped water over her breakfast plate. "Count 'em. Eighteen years of goading that shiftless sumbitch into being somebody, into shooting fer the big record money. The Opry an all that mess. I sat at enough teensie tables in Kentucky, Tennessee, goddam Georgia pool halls, long electric nights enough to contract epidermal eruptions and an allergy to sawdust."

"My word," Myrna boggled, chin in hand.

Kate still gazed out the crystal-flaked panes

while showing the kitchen an ample butt of her own. Aunt Floy made bad coffee full of grits and those deer would be lucky to make it to the trees if Aunt Floy wasn't already cleaning up her big breakfast.

"Everbody dances to Lovell, honey, but *he don't listen* to nobody, nothin, not never, not ever," Floy advised her younger nieces. "He don't never mind his Lady Floy at all. I told him to drop that jungle bunny shit and pick hillbilly like they want on Music Row. Nobody wants to cut no wax on that jungle bunny shit. Christ, Lovell I'd say, only white folks is gonna buy enough platters to bankroll our swim pool. The coloreds ain't gonna git you no pink tailfins or silk suits. Slow them tunes down, baby, I said. Mebbe Ernest Tubb will take you on as a Troubadour, then you kin work yer way up the ladder with that Jim Denny who books the Opry. Hmmmph. Know what your Uncle Lovell said to that, Myrna honey?"

"Garsh, I dunno. What?"

"Plug me in you split-tailed shrew."

Kate roared, laughing herself sick as she fell against the window. Floy frowned at her. Myrna's chins and blond ringlets shook, a wry spasm on her lips. She covered it quick with her hand, afraid to join her sister's folly.

"But Uncle Love sockin' them electric blues is what caught *yer* fancy. Didn't he now?" Kate said darkly, all smiles now. She liked that shit Auntie called jungle bunny shit.

Their three-hundred-pound queen bee took offense. "You young and ignorant, Miss Myrna. Lady Floy wasn't always lit with grace. She was a fool thing once herself. A finger-poppin', panty-twistin' fool. But not fer long."

"Made a couple of records though, didn't he, Aintie Floy?" Myrna kept smirking.

"A couple. Damn his hide," Floy snapped, kicking off her fuzzy houseslippers. She did not care for little Miss Myrna's tone. "My fancy, *my foot*. Where's he hid out? They's only a hunert and twenty skins left in my china kitty."

Kate sighed, wise beyond her years. "He's got moxie, Uncle does. Always comes home after a day or two."

"A day or two, smarty Kate, that's right. Never been gone *five days* before. This is day five. I swear, if Lovell Starling brings me home that bloody pox what's been eatin' up ever Mutt, Jeff and scar-kissed Lych who spooks at the sight of bathwater—I mean—*last thing* we need. Damn, I'm blue. Feel like shopping up a little good cheer. How'z about you darlins running me into Ewe Spring, mebbe even Cayuga Ridge, to pick out a few things?"

Myrna shrugged. "Sure, Aintie Floy. You bet. Paw-Paw's done fed and so is the stock."

"Deeelightful," Floy rang, squeezing out through her kitchen door. "Let me jist buff my toenails and

I'll be right with you. Law, mebbe we'll buy you each a perty-perty hair barrette or somethin'."

Floy buffed the pointy toenails she had just lacquered crimson the night before. She found her good high heels and frayed mohair car coat. Both girls held Auntie's outstretched hands like Floy was a great and gangly stuffed stork picking her way through the snow to their tractor. Floy sat backwards on the hydraulic hitch while Kate perched on the wide left fender. Kate drove responsibly, as always.

Lady Floy watched snowy hillsides unreel behind her, giving way to glazed asphalt when they reached the road. Her footsies were freezing in the glittery, open-toed shoes, but Floy had learned to live with it. Beauty exacted its price.

They stopped at Miss Doobelle's, where Floy left a Butterick pattern and her down-payment on a new orchid chiffon dinner gown before they went on up the branch to Ewe Springs. She selected some magazines and lipsticks (but no barrettes) from Valentine's Salon, sat for one of Valentine's Tulip waves, then Floy bought dinner for herself and the girls at The Brass Dray Inn; a smoked goose and fixings which the three decimated in five minutes. After dinner, the well-fed trio rode the diesel tractor over to Cayuga Ridge. Once there, Floy could not find the brand of pear halves she desired from Birdnell's Mercantile Feed, Fuel & Grain. She had made a special trip for those pears, her syrupy favorites.

"Where's my special favorite pears, Mr. Willy? This ain't them," her shrill demanded, hoisting an inferior brand betwixt plump thumb and forefinger.

"And I *am* most sorry Mizz Floy," said Willy, behind the candy jars, eager to please. "They couldn't ship no Sunnybowl Pears this week. A trucker strike or something like that. I hear them Hi-Lo Pears yer a-holdin' make mighty fine eats, though."

Floy set the pears back on the shelf. "I tell you what, Mr. Willy. When Sunnybowl returns to your establishment my sugar pear dollars will return as well. Gimme some of them peppermints anyhow, and I'll take this comb set and this here scarf. Oh, and some of that Sal Hepatica purgative."

She peeled off one battered green bill after another. As always, Floy did her best not to think about all the grimy hillbilly hands that had handled this money the Axman brought home. It still spent like new, she told herself. Birdnell's array of perty-perty hair barrettes appealed to Myrna and Kate no more than those back at Valentine's Salon, meaning—not remotely on their hairiest day. So Floy bought them a case of Chocolate Soldier and left it at that.

"How's ole Lovell that gitpickin ace these days?" Willy joshed as they left his store.

"He's dead or better be, Willy. Now shuddup."

The afternoon was waning, so the girls took Floy back home after Cayuga Ridge. Snow began filtering through the late grey light as they helped her inside with her purchases. They left right after that and Floy felt a whole lot better. Pretty soon, breakfast and dinner began to move on her, making her wonder for the umpteenth time how her Uncle Dodge (Kate and Myrna's grandpaw who lent Floy this shotgun palace) could have brains enough to string the place with rural electric but still have no proper plumbing.

The tooth tore loose. Floy wrapped it preciously and finished her business, using the soft tissues she brought from the house. No Monkey Wards wipes for Lady Floy. But now there was an open pit festering back there in her gum. Her poor and sorely pit thirsted for some cherry wine. Fortunately, half a pint was still lukewarm in her lingerie drawer. Worse still and even more sorely open—was Floy herself. She was *really* hankering after— some deep nookie. Lovell wasn't too interested in her deep nookie these days. More often than not, after she rolled the skunk-drunk gitpicker for his folding money, she had to pin him down, hike her skirt and overload that nookie for herself.

This desire nipped at Floy. She evacuated the skin-tight privy, going back inside to her cozy boudoir where the Rotogravure magazine wallpaper gave her scads to think about. After a few hours of sipping cherry wine she took care of her own dern nookie. When she got right down to it, Floy's nookie

needed no help from Mister Lovell Starling, thank you very much.

Fionuala Brynn Dar'bannon was dreaming silver again. She was forever dreaming silver, remembering silvery days in a silvery light. Perhaps it was because glints of silver were the sharpest she could still see, dreaming or awake.

But she was surely dreaming now.

Fionuala could glean that much.

She was surely dreaming, surely dreaming now.

She was riding in the catfish car with Mrs. Kleef at the wheel. Mrs. Kleef drove a mud-grey car that looked like a slow, slimy catfish. With silver whiskers. Fionuala might have left Mrs. Kleef behind lifetimes ago but Mrs. Kleef never left one's dreams for long.

"Do you read us, missy?" Mrs. Kleef was asking.

Who was us? They were always alone on this mountain road. In a silver wash of metallic sunlight, Fionuala looked over at Mrs. Kleef who also had whiskers. A thin, furry mustache feathered Mrs. Kleef's upper lip, the squat woman peering over big knuckles on a big steering wheel. Mrs. Kleef's hammertoe rode the gas pedal. Fionuala gazed out the window at shining, silvery treetops brushing past them, the chipper twinkle of wrens on air. She nudged her mirror spectacles back into place. Fionuala was wearing the same polka-dot smock that fit her on the trip down to the home two years before. She had not worn it since. Familiar, she thought, how familiar.

"Do you read us, missy?" Mrs. Kleef repeated, eyes still latched on the shimmering route ahead.

Fionuala felt herself nod.

"Do you read us?"

Silver currents of light flowed from the rearview mirror, speckled with soft, giggling voices—they curled around Mrs. Kleef, wrapping around her bulb-shaped head before light and giggles streamed out the open window, trailing far behind the catfish car. Fionuala felt nice. She was happy. She was going home.

"You're not ready, you know. Not ready for a real world full of real peoples." Mrs. Kleef kept talking to Mrs. Kleef's big knuckles. "Real peoples lie and steal and some will take advantage of a girl like you. Some will take advantage. Some will take advantage and you've not been much of a problem to us at the home, but your father wants you back and some will take advantage and he's got a pot of money but he say we can't keep you anymore..."

Same old Mrs. Kleef. Same old hammertoe. Same old dream.

"...even though our little missy is not ready-or-not for real peoples."

Asininity. That's what this dream woman was. Fionuala spake only to herself during the entire journey home. She did not answer back *then* and she would never respond to such nonsense *now*, not in this silvery situation. She was waiting to speak with Asta, her father, her only adult visitor in the last two years. Dear Asta—whom she never called Daddy—who wanted his girl back, now that Asta's wife was dead and mailing no hospital checks.

"My word, Fionuala Brynn, you're growing like a shoot."

Fionuala's specs looked again. Now, it was father, Asta Dar'bannon, driving. Mrs. Kleef was memory. The catfish car was memory. Of course, Mr. Dar'bannon was memory, too. In memory, Asta sat silver-haired, straight and well-groomed while guiding the great Royale Victoria. "...growing, growing, growing like a shoot."

"Am I?" Fionuala asked in return.

"Yes, indeed you are. You've blossomed into young womanhood and I know why."

"Tell me why, Asta, tell me why." Why had she never called him Daddy?

"Because the world outside our familial walls has awakened you. Sunshine, A—Bombs, spring showers and Mars bars—enhanced by the cultural refinements gained within our home, naturally. Naturally. No more secret whisperings, dead languages, no more ghostly companions. I am only sad that your mother cannot see her young lady flourish."

Fionuala thought about Asta's wife for a fraction.

"I am too, Asta. I'm sad too."

Asta's finely beveled nails splayed at the windshield.

"Oh darling, we're home in time for tea," her father lilted.

Fionuala looked and saw the grand shining house, weepy willows dripping with sparkly tinsel, just like Christmas. The garden was alive, truly alive, zinging a joyful springtime tune.

The Royale Victoria drove up the steps and into the foyer. They drove once around the parlor then up the staircase, passing through Fionuala's old room with the nursery carol wallpaper. The Royale Victoria rode the dumb waiter down to their gleaming, utensil-draped kitchen.

"Soon you will be mature enough to drive yourself," Asta told her as they wheeled through the library, then into her parent's regal bedchamber. Asta's wife lay within the bedposts, a face of rice paper, half-sewn into her shroud. Fionuala snuck a smile when their Royale Victoria left the chamber then turned left toward the back porch.

As fat tires rumbled out the backdoor, down the stoop, Fionuala saw her own plain fingers on the ivory steering wheel. She was driving herself now, this was no Royale Victoria and the sky was silver foil, rippling. She released the wheel, turned around in the seat. The hearse's long compartment held Asta's glass casket. Asta lay perfectly tailored inside the glass, open-eyed and consumptive. He was beautiful under glass. Fionuala scooted back around, retook the wheel of her rolling hearse. The rearview mirror giggled and spake as Fionuala reflected on the line of putt-putt cars trailing behind her, headed for the silver-stoned cemetery. She felt happy. Asta was going home.

Then her shining dream went white, snowy white, as she rounded a frozen curve and saw the darkling fellow. A tall fellow with a silver-stringed guitar.

The Axman propped up on white cotton sheets, all the better to study Fina's foot. She needed one foot protruding while she slept, as though her five dainty toes required liberation from smothering coverlets, no matter how cold the night. Why, this very morning was early, grey and rising warm, but he knew those tiny toes were still chilly to the touch.

Lovell loved the arch of her foot. There was a spare, fledgling grace to that arch. He spent many, many daybreaks lusting after it. Over there, his guitar leaned against the mahogany wardrobe, waiting for him. He thought about strumming his cat-strings for that arch. He considered composing an ode to that arch, but did not wish to waken Fina from her dreams. He tugged the sheet, revealing more of her milky ankle. He favored the ankle too: he loved to taste the ankle, to kiss it until she got giddy. But nothing compared to her naked arch. Her toes flicked away a lazy fly, a pleasing sight to the connoisseur.

He was growling hungry. Lovell lay back in bed and considered rolling some laughing tobacco to cleanse his palate. He had abandoned most every other abuse. But he liked to roll smoke. He liked the fresh musk of it. He liked handling the mealy paper, the skill and dexterity of the roll, plus, it staved off his appetite for a short while. And buttery flapjacks would taste that much richer, once Fina was awake.

Every bit of this was rumination, of course. His butt didn't move. The sky didn't fall quite yet. The smoke would wait, just like his guitar. He seemed to get deep pleasure doing next to nothing these days. Pondering footsies and the morning's heat and bedroom canopies were just about his speed. Built for comfort, baby, not for speed. Maybe there was a chorus bubbling up, searching for a vamp. Maybe he and axe #1 would work out that vamp. Maybe trolls camped inside this mattress. Lovell wondered if he could ever orientate to such a vast chunk of bed as this bed, muchless the very *idea* of a—what would Floy call it?—a *boudoir* the size of this haybarn of a boudoir. Fina's shaded glasses looked back at him from her 17th-century Acanthus bedstand. She kept his mind off these quiet splendors most of the time, but Lovell doubted he would ever take it in stride. Still, he felt more dozy than wise anymore, and he caught himself smiling over dribs and drabs.

When Lovell saw her straight-eight Royale Victoria locomoting long and low along the snowpack that hard glacial morning, he wasn't so dozy. He was just hungover. A pill-percolated beer hungover, which was always the worst. Meaning, his headache stole the show that morning more than his troubled heart and mind. He did not want company.

No matter, here came company, ready or not. Lovell stood shivering on Six Bucket Run, eyeing the blindered Reo as it slowed on the road alongside him. Weird, man, he thought. Weird. All it needed was a shepherd dog and white cane. Lovell could not see inside the car. The Royale Vic's windows were tinted midnight swamp green. His inner ear crackled with rancor. He shoved a fist into his coat pocket, cupping the straight razor tucked there, in case of a fracas.

Little in life, very little, prepared him for the bird that emerged that frigid day. The driver's door clicked open. She flapped out like a lame and hooded peacock blanching at sudden sunlight. Whatsmore, she wore the sappiest puss he had ever seen. For that matter, her puss was *all* you could see. Ultra-dark sunglasses peered from under a ten-gallon sunhat, anchored to her chin by her sheer black scarf. White gloves met fitted knit sleeves, then disappeared into the deep folds of her widow's weeds, an antiquarian brocade left over from another century. Despite this camouflage, Lovell sensed a frail frame lurking under her pleated armor. Her only exposed flesh was a dainty chin and plucky smile.

"Mmmmmm, my" she mused. "What an exotic instrument."

She almost whispered, an airy voice, an echo with no point of origin.

It was then Lovell realized she was addressing his axe. Those big sunshades didn't give up much. Who knew where her eyes were going? She sure wasn't much of a looker under all that garb, he could readily tell.

"Never seen a gitfiddle before, ma'am?" Lovell coughed, releasing the razor in his pocket. He suspected she was ten, fifteen years his junior.

"A git—fiddle. Why, no. Do you stroke it like a cello? Does it come with a horsehair bow?" Her voice broke pleasantly, almost gigging his funny bone.

"Naw, ma'am, it's a guitar. You know, a *guitar.*"

"Yesss, I have seen a guitar from time to time. In catalogues. But yours has a peculiar apparatus attached, if I am not mistaken. Are those radio knobs down there?" she asked, pointing.

Lovell slung the axe off his back.

"Nope. It's jist an eee-lectric guitar. Made this

one myself."

"Electric..." she nodded, cupping the word in her small mouth. "An electrical guitar. How very clever, simply startling. What, exactly, does this electricity *do* for the instrument?"

"Do?"

"Does it light up? Or play songs on a paper music roll? Like our automatic piano?"

Lovell snickered finally. You had to dig it. It was too, too gone. Lovell swiftly divorced all thoughts of that house—Floy's house—Floy's Uncle Dodge's house. It had never been home to Lovell. Floy could sit tight.

"Naw, nothin like that. No Christmas lights. That voltage, it jist kicks my chords up louder and kinda queers the sound. Charges it up, you might say. Better fer the boogie."

"*Boogie?!*" Her milky lips gasped recognition. "Our piano plays the Beale Street Boogie. Plays it very nicely, yes, I would say it is my favorite. Asta, my beloved father—he purchased the roll but his wife called it an abomination, forcing Asta to store it inside the piano seat."

"I doubt it's the same woof of boogie I'm prone to bop."

She giggled at him.

"*Kai shen aroe.* Your language is delightful. Do you plug it in?"

"Plug in my language?"

"Your gitfiddler, is it? Do you plug it into an out-let proper, into the wall fixture?"

He shook his dull head, hit a lick on the sil-ver-stringed box. Thin and soft, it bit the air, like a thin steel shiv.

"Not the axe—ummm—not the insturment itself. I jist wall-plug the amplifier."

She did not ask about the amplifier and he ap-preciated that. She knew when to skip ahead. Lovell ducked his lashes, testing her open admiration.

"Why the quiz show?" he probed.

"Oh. Élan. Élan is the staff of my existence. I am seldom able to leave my home, so my élan is ofttimes confined to shifts of moonlight and season, ladybugs on my African violets, that sort of thing." The ten-gal-lon sunhat cocked up at him—dark, blank glasses unmoving over her sallow cheeks. Tiny wrinkles were just sprouting along the ridge of her upper lip. Perhaps she was older than he first thought.

"Why you cover yerself so?" Lovell did not stutter.

She sighed, eagerly, appreciating his candor.

"Isn't it wickedly absurd? An affront to one's nat-ural eye?" she demanded with husky fervor, showing small, even teeth that radiated something a tad—well, electric. "I cannot suffer any harsh sun due to my condition. I am afraid mine is an extremely rare, systemic condition that leaves me debilitated and homebound much of the time. Too much di-rect sunlight can aggravate, even *activate* the worst symptoms, causing a flare-up which might leave me bedridden for days, even weeks. I am resoundingly incurable. I have borne it for years and keep chugging along. So no pity for Fionuala Dar'bannon, thank you. My eyes are particularly sensitive."

"Damn, that was a snootful." Lovell leaned against her Royale Victoria, strangely comforted by this bird and her plight. Her condition, whatever it was, did not resemble the pestilent skin eruptions or blood disturbance that was worming its way through the local backwoods of late. She looked certifiable, yes. But she hardly looked contagious.

"Speaking of electricalities..."

Were they, he wondered? Were they speaking of electricalities?

"Perhaps you are aware of some handy fellow or tradesman fluent with the alternating current," she continued. "Not the directing current, I was told, the alternating one. My lights went out during our horrendous blow last night. I lit the hurricane lamps. The furnace is ripe with oil, thank goodness. But otherwise I am in a pickle."

Lovell scratched his beard, grinning with her. She set a gloved hand on the fender alongside his.

"Why, the whole *morning* has been a pickle. My housekeeper, Ess, she sent her little colored boy over first thing before breakfast to tell me she was tending a horrid tummy ache and could not shop my groceries or clean. I rely upon Ess for most of my outside errands, you see. At present, I am feeling my way toward Cayuga Ridge. Is the road passable?"

"Prob'ly not."

"I thought the Cayuga school janitor might be acquainted with super power surges and other electricalities. Do you know him?"

"No, ma'am, I do not. Prob'ly a fuse would fix you."

"Yes, a fuse," she enthused, perfectly ungrasping.

He asked and she told him there were no downed lines in her yard. Since power was still live back at the lounge he suspected her fuse box. And not surprisingly, Lovell's boots wanted in from the cold and damp. The prospect of Floy's hard homecoming had blown off into the arctic oblivion.

Behind her blind shades, this odd Royale Victorian woman got fiercely ecstatic when Lovell said, "I kin do a fuse. Any damn beau kin do a damn fuse."

So, she took him home.

He spent the trip making peace with her eight-piston cocoon. It was calming. The Reo's tinted windows cut the sun's glare by half, creating a greenish cell. Lovell had never felt the like. His ass unpuckered. She was a cautious driver. Soon he forgot about deadly roadslides or patches of black ice. He was ready to go. Along the way, she told him to call her Fina. Just call her Fina, she mewed. Her friends did.

Home was some-kind-of-swank alright. Jumbo-sized and special as finding Notre Dame Cathedral shut off, towering up a run amidst snow-peaked regency. Lovell had seen this one before. In the National Geographic.

"Home again, home again, jiggityjig," she trilled.

When she finally idled along that stretch of brown-vined arbor into the receiving end of a swell carriage house, Lovell got tongue-sprung. Icicle nests circled in formation around the arbor; a crystalline garden sprouting behind low stone walls and latticework, mired in windswept drifts, neglected and complete with its own frozen puddle-duck pond. A commanding shade turned the duckless ice purple, the three-story, pavilion-peaked shade of that splendor she called home again, home again. Freshly salted tiles led their way, climbing inevitably toward the manor house's broad, riverstone foundation. Before they made the porch, Lovell tried but failed to count each of those steep-gabled dormers above, totaling up the silent windows that watched him come. Cradling his raunchy guitar, he was given, strangely given, to counting her steeples. The simple task was stabilizing.

Her indoors was everything he should have expected at this point. Cornices and high ceilings, room after epic room, landscapes under glass, formal portraits in rich oils, murky hallways, depthless corners, velveteen loveseats and scrolled woodgrains that whispered money, money, money. She gushed appreciation, for Lovell, for the stringed instrument, the automatic piano in her parlor, The Holy Encyclopedia Brittanica, crickets, and other passing interests which he lost track of as they zig-zagged through labyrinthine chambers. He noticed an overabundance of snapshots. Every doily and lampstand held a postcard or three, or four, a stereoscopic slide, a foreign postage stamp, a ripple-edge photo. No matter where his eye fell, he saw Carlesbad Caverns or the Colossus Of Rhodes. Stereo-visions of The Great San Francisco Earthquake scattered across a footstool.

Eventually, Lovell found the laundry porch where he found the problem in her circuit box. He proved true. Lovell fixed her blown fuse, gave her the juice and when he returned to her parlor with the nine-bulb chandelier all aglow, her veils had lifted.

She ran, clasped his coat sleeve and gushed, "Transcendent is the light!"

She spun, hands high. He gave a chuckle.

"Light, oh light, *espathen teke jind uava de tosh!*

"*Espa—?*"

"The Gaelic means: of dying embers the spirit shines. A friend taught me as a child."

Yes, Miss Fionuala had shed her wraps, and was soon explaining volumes about her very weak eyes. He saw she was willowy and fragile indeed, a network of freckles upon lucid skin. No more dark glasses. Her swollen brown eyes were revealed, her crop of ash-auburn curls. Fionuala Dar'bannon thanked him mercilessly. She reminded Lovell of a space alien he had seen one Saturday matinee. No, this one was hardly the looker from where he stood. And here, under the unvarnished glare of her chandelier, Lovell figured Miss Dar'bannon had waved bye-bye to thirty-five, maybe even forty, though she could fake ten years up or down. Her eyes were dimming, she said, weak and dimming with each day.

There was no coffee, so she served him warm cocoa in a sun-drenched glass nook she called the Florida room. They sat at a round teakwood table and drank from gilt-edged teacups.

"You'll need a proper fuse from the hardware. Made do with a copper penny in the meantime," Lovell admitted, stroking his devilish spade beard.

"How clever. A copper penny. You can do such a thing?"

"Legions have. But swap it back or you might burn this Taj Mahal down." He took pause, meeting her liquid brown gaze. She was beaming back at him from the shade of a rubber tree plant. His eardrum hit a rimshot. "Anyway, shut yer gate, the meter's runnin. Miss Fina's back on rural electric. Is she happy then?"

He was beginning to speak her language.

"Wickedly warm and wickedly happy," her airy, fluted tongue told him, more cocoa pouring forth, "are you happy Mr. Starling?"

"Happier than a sissy in a C.C.C. camp."

Fionuala giggled, though she had no notion of what he meant and he knew it and she knew he knew. She did not really grasp his language yet. But somehow, nothing in the words really mattered. She asked if he had a home and he said not really. She asked if he was married. Lovell answered the same. He described the roadhouse, the music he made there, the drunken ovations he had provoked in so many joints for so many years. They all seemed phony in the telling. But she listened with swollen-eyed rapture.

He slept the night in a spare bedroom. She insisted. He insisted. It would just be for a few days. Before he moved in, though, Lovell borrowed her Royale Vic to fetch his guitar amp and motorcycle from Bull's Gladiola Lounge. The car got through, but not without adventure. Lovell left Bull a note saying he figured Saturday night was no-go what with these slick roads so the Axman was heading south to flamingo heaven: Bull would need a new headliner. Lovell didn't jot a dot about Floy. During his dusky return, the weather thickened into stiff snow flurries. Arriving with a bumper-load of Indian Scout motorbike, Lovell parked inside then fought the carriage house doors closed. Winter's dark sank fast. Fionuala's white castle accepted him once more.

Blissful, he snoozed like a mole in his splendid guest room, snow deepening throughout the night.

Down the second-floor hallway, Fionuala slept in her own little room with the nursery carol wallpaper.

Next morning, Lovell sipped cocoa, told some war stories from the road, then tuned an E-string up to D so he could pick and sing a couple of jump tunes for Miss Dar'bannon. This seemed to excite her. Taking his hand, she led him on a more extensive tour through her vast manor. He quickly learned the lay of the house, including which toilet pipes complained, access to the rooftop cupola, the total number of gables: twelve. There was even a secret staircase behind a panel in the second-floor linen closet. Pure Abbott and Costello stuff. The cramped, hidden steps descended to the furnace cellar where you could exit the house from flat double storm doors—if you could lift two feet of snow. The third floor was currently unfurnished, given over long since to dust and storage. Eventually, Fionuala grew faint, so she napped several hours of the afternoon while Lovell repaired a library shelf, then leaned out a third-story alcove and lag-bolted the shaky lightning rod to the house's crown. For supper he made his Mad Rabbit Stew, going easy on the red pepper for the sake of his host's delicate stomach. He whipped up a bowl of snow ice cream as an antidote, drizzling caramel over it before delivery. Licking spoons, they shared slides and postcards she solicited faithfully from around the world. Her swollen eyes ached to see all wondrous sights and vistas, she said, before her eyes were gone. "How long?" he asked. Months, maybe years, she could not say. The snow held for most of the coming week. The housekeeper never appeared.

During his third night, Fionuala came to the guest room and woke Lovell. He returned with her to the little rhyme-papered room where he took her virginity. After that, they made love every night and every morning before cocoa. There was nothing said about it. Fionuala accepted him and his presence within her as though Lovell had simply reappeared from some mislaid remembrance when their hearts and bodies had once entwined. With each kiss, her true loveliness surfaced and he saw. How could he have overlooked such fair beauty? So what if, from time to time, he overheard her speaking something she called Gaelic to the mirrors and clocks. She was used to living alone, where her natural charms had suffered from lack of appreciation. His beard left a mild rash on her cheeks, her belly, her legs. She did not mind, but he shaved the beard anyway. In lush tones, she declared him the handsome rake, with or without his shrubbery.

For a week he strummed her and his guitar while Fionuala's naps grew shorter. After dark, they built fires in the library's hearth where she lay before him, growing warm, pink, strong. He held each darling foot in hand. Her naked arch seduced his everloving soul. Outside, the snow began to thaw.

When Ess the housekeeper brought groceries that following Saturday, Fionuala cut the lady's workload by half, getting her out of the place in under two hours while Lovell hid behind the secret panel upstairs. He sat inside the wall on the tight, candle-lit stair, sketching erotic figures in a Big Chief notebook until he heard Fionuala's gentle tap from the linen closet, her airy flute trilling, "*aelspin frey ma tein, woen ma*...come out, come out, my love. Wherever you are, you are for *meee-heeee*."

Winter surrendered to mayapples, wysteria and Queen Anne's lace. Lovell kept a low profile, working the garden when nobody was around—which was almost always. Who were these friends who called her Fina? Rarely, it crossed his mind. Where were these friends? There was the housekeeper twice a week. An old family lawyer visited monthly, bringing stipends from the Roanoke bank, discussing vague executory matters in her parlor while Lovell stayed upstairs. This gave him time to plan his attack on the horticultural front. He began to draft a free-standing belvedere (for shade-sitting) on lined tablet paper. Yes, one had to wonder, but rarely.

Lovell dredged the duck pond with twin pitchforks strapped together, wading knee-deep, clearing out weeds while Fina sat on the porch viewing three-dimensionals through her stereoscope. Once done, Lovell was proud of the unclogged pond. Given time, some duck might even call Lovell's watery handiwork a home. He tilled fresh rows at the back of the garden, invisible behind evergreen spires. These rows he planted with laughing tobacco and crowder peas. Lovell had always been partial to crowder peas. Meat was plentiful. The neighboring forest was so untapped, he could hunt fowl or rabbit from the porch. Fina's daddy, Asta, provided a fine Marlin Rimfire rifle from his collection.

One Tuesday in late August, the narrow staircase had gotten altogether too damn hot and stifling when restless Lovell thought he heard housekeeper Ess crank up her old Dodge to leave. He was just reaching for the secret panel's handle—when Ess began mumbling a few inches from his face, on the other side.

"So how much was it, mister?" he heard her ask softly, in a voice deep as any bullfrog's. "Let's see. It run sixteen and four bits—and two penny. Sixteen from twenty, that's, uh—"

Lovell went rigid. Ess was a breath away from him, inside the linen closet, only the panel betwixt them.

"—that's *four* dollar. Four bits from a dollar, that's four bits more—"

She was talking to herself. He heard the housekeeper pull clean sheets from the shelves. Lovell got stranger than wise, afraid to move off down the stair, afraid Ess might hear the creak of steps inside the wall.

"—then there's the two penny. That leaves forty, forty, forty-*sebbum*. Yes, ma'am. She owe me three dollar and forty-sebbum cent."

He didn't even know what Miss Ess looked like. He had never seen her clearly. He wished she would go away. Ess slid a blanket from its berth, somewhere near Lovell's ankles. The floor flexed as she left the closet. Pressing his mended ear to the wall, her one-woman debate continued down the hall toward Fionuala's bedroom. Lovell realized it was only grocery change Ess was ciphering. Only change due her for the tally. Faintly now, the trickle of Fina's laughter came up through the boards, joined by gleeful chimes from Ess's youngest boy, Melrose—who came with the housekeeper when school was out.

Lovell slumped back down on his step, damp in the head.

When Fionuala heard about this close call she declared it Pickwickian, that's right, poppycock incarnate, as she leapt into his arms. The following Saturday she paid Ess a fifty-dollar bonus, then sent her home for the last time. The housekeeper's long, steadfast service was no longer required. Fina said Ess was perplexed but took it in her usual stride.

It was the right way to go. They were independent-minded people. Their house took care of itself. She seldom took her naps anymore, though she was still sun-sensitive and always would be. Lovell cooked, making the occasional sugar and supply run into Ewe Springs where he was less known. He would park her clashingly-tinted Royale Victoria somewhere out of the way, usually down a blind alley, then walk up the lane to shop. Once he ran into a hillbilly jump fan who knew him from the club, a boy named Percy—but Lovell was more easy talking by then and did not really mind the encounter. Another time, in the blind alley, he crossed paths with a long, old, preacher-looking thing who asked him how went a tizzypoke? That's what the long thing demanded. How went a tizzypoke? This encounter was not to Lovell's liking. But he let it go. He kept on walking.

Later that day, he stumbled across Winston's Musical Instrument Emporium, newly-opened, where Lovell bought himself a new D-string before heading home to his Fina. With his amp barely humming, he played her every scarlet torch song, every sweetheart's lament he knew. Later they made love in her parent's great canopied bed for the first time, with all the windows open, with crickets and scent of hydrangea tickling over fleshly pleasures. From that evening forward the great vaulted bedroom was theirs.

At Fionuala's urging, they began to make daylong excursions in the Royale Victoria Reo. She would don her layers and dark glasses then Lovell locomoted slowly out of the hills, sometimes to Roanoke, sometimes as far as Shepville for a Saturday picture show. She liked Mr. Montgomery Clift. He liked Miss Barbara Stanwyck. They both loved *King Solomon's Mines*. They spent hours turning Rexall's postcard rack, haunting museums and record shops. They even rode a Ferris wheel under cloudy skies. It was even easier to stock their groceries in bulk in downland Roanoke or Shepville then carry the booty home. There was much to choose from in the city. Yet, it always felt great to escape the city clatter at day's end.

Only once did Fionuala seem vexed. One autumn afternoon, with sunset near, they left Roanoke and headed back for the hills. Bridge repairs forced Lovell to detour the Royale Victoria, cruising past the silver gate and silvery lawns of St. Dympna's Healing Home. Fina averted her gaze, turned inside herself, and played possum during the return trip. Usually she chattered non-stop. But that day, with the sun ebbing through swamp-green glass, Lovell left her to her secrets. He was much the same as she. So be it.

Lovell wouldn't know real Gaelic if the words were etched in stone. So who the hell cared if her Gaelic was blarney? There had been no skin rashes nor irritable reactions to sunlight—not in months. If her swollen eyes had weakened, Lovell was unaware. Apparently, so far, Fina saw as sharply as ever. Perhaps too sharply. She still doted on her stereoscope and exotic photos. And Lovell, he had his own fetish for Taj Mahals. He was just learning how to look, to look out, not in; for his own mysteries shone brightest in Fina's celestial eyes. She made him tougher every day. Tougher than wise.

A year went dawdling by. They grew pokier together, weathered more snow storms and now it was red-hot August again, waiting for the flames to break. Waiting for cool relief.

Lovell savored her naked arch for that extra moment, licked Fionuala's tasty nape before leaving bed. He took the translation of Gabriele D'Annunzio's *The Flame Of Life* from his bedstand, retiring to the porcelain throne for further study. Afterward, he made for the kitchen. Lovell held cocoa in high favor, especially Fina's cocoa. But two of the loveliest new arrivals in their home, dearest to Lovell's heart, were chicory and roasted beans in the cupboard.

What to conjure for breakfast, what would delight her, he wondered? Wearing canary silk bottoms (and only canary silk bottoms) Lovell padded through the marbled foyer, smelling phantasmic pecan muffins in his near future. Passing the front door, he chanced a glance out the door's prismed glass. Lovell was caught short by what he saw, stopping to gaze.

Bent in the prism, a big, big man was coming

up the gloamy path. Moving from inside the arbor where Lovell's Indian motorcycle was now stashed. The man was grimy, barefoot in a flimsy blue nightie.

That man was Floy.

Quietly, Lovell slipped out, latching the door closed. Son-of-a-bitch-born-Satan if it wasn't Floy. She was big, but he had seen her bigger. Every big inch of her, he'd felt that inch, he'd smelt that inch, he'd been pinned flat by that inch, he'd left his climaxes in their bargain. And her inches had all been bigger. This morning, loose skin-flaps draped off Lady Floy's bulk. Something was awry with her hairdo. Floy spotted him but gave nothing away. She looked unhealthy in her torn, shapeless nightie. Why, Lovell figured, she couldn't weigh more than two hundred and a quarter.

"Mornin', doll. How ya been...?" Her mouth sounded boggy, aimless.

"Mornin' to you, Floy."

Floy accepted this new reality. She had found him. Him, or some fool who could pass for the late Lovell Starling. Perhaps here was a stranger who only looked the part. What could she expect? Floy climbed the porch, sat on the swing. Their faces never quite met. Then the floodgates blew open. Floy began to bay and bawl, horribly. Lovell fretted as her tears rolled on. Mainly, he fretted about waking Fionuala.

"You never did come home, doll," she snuffled finally.

He sat on the porch rail and faced up to her while looking down. "This, mmm...this here's my home now."

"But you din't come back to yer Lady Floy."

"No. I did not."

Her wet chin quaked, dropping open. More teeth had been lost. Suddenly her eyes pled up at him.

"I'm yer *wife*. Best come home with yer wife now."

"We was never married proper," he shook his head. "You know that."

"But, all our years of struggle and strife..."

"Married or not, them years is over. Thank God and Billy Sunday."

"Wooo-w-was-was-was ever bit so b-b-bad?"

"No. Not ever bit."

Floy's cheeks pooched out, about to bust as her mind drifted off, across the mist-couched lawn where bright sunrise was overdue. Lovell's heart sank. She had never left her boudoir without three coats of semi-gloss, not in all their years together. He could clearly see the ragged complexion, the ill-plucked eyebrows. Her hair hung limp and spongy, matted with hairspray, clinging with lint, sticker burrs and crap. Shoeless, her chipped gold toenails begged for soap and a trim. But her wasting corpse could *not* figure in this conversation. Lovell had little choice. He had nothing left to give her.

"Lady's been workin..."

"That's fine. That's good."

"Been pickin' fruit fer Uncle Dodge an friends of his. Moppin' an sweepin' up fer Bull sometimes. Bull, he said you left him a bye-bye note. I said, Axman din't leave me no bye-bye note..."

Lovell shut his eyes, aching to blot out her woes. For Mister Pity's sake, he wanted to ask Floy, do we have to do this? Can't you just fix yourself sexy again? Can't you snare another thumb picker? Why not settle for a burlycue piano man, or an elderly pedal-steel man ripe for his Navy pension? Christ, wasn't there some fool barkeep, somewhere, with a grubstake and a footlong, rock-hard death wish? But Lovell did not ask. His eyes opened and looked, out. Sizing her up, he saw enough.   She was still talking.

"...Run into dumb ole kid pitching pennies front of Ewe Spring merchant establishment. Done sold my rooty-toot shoes an jewelry, ain't I? So that dumb ole kid says he sees ya driving this Reo and kid tells me *who* that Reo belongs to. Folks say she's daft from a *early* age, yes, they do."

"She's not daft," Lovell shot back, arms crossing his bare chest.

"She perty? Pertier than me?"

"Leave her go, Floy. She's a good woman."

"You love her, don't ya, doll?"

He nodded.

"I git scary up at the place. Alone..."

"I'm sorry."

"Last week," she reached out, touched his knee, then withdrew the hand, "last week I believe it was, after midnight. I woke up, sweaty and hot, hearing voices out back around the clothesline. Lych voices. I heard that mush right off. Ain't I heard Lych voices before?"

Her words got low. In the dank light, Lovell could see the huge medallions of Floy's nipples through her thin, blue batista gown. An old bloody crust stained the collar's hem, a stray spit of red beside her left nipple.

"Got out the bucklight, shined it out the back window and I saw em. Two Lych's alright. Long man and a long woman. I could see them messy faces of theirs, even from the house, and she was round-bellied, ready to drop— as you will soon see. I hollered scat and they both run off into the wood, uphill of the privy. Couldn't sleep after that of course. An hour or two, and she commences to wail. Up there in the trees. Serious wailing, terrible wailing and screeches through the night. Every so often I caught wind of him too, that Lych feller coaxin' her through it, kind of soft and steady in words nobody fit could understand.

"They was gone the next afternoon when I finally felt sturdy enough to search the wood. Didn't take long to find it. That dead suckling they had left behind, unburied. Right betwixt two sassafras roots it lay, still half-stuck in its afterbirth. Couldn't tell if it was a he or a she Lych." Floy threw Lovell a wild, unfixed stare. "Lovell, that Lych suckling, it had that bloody pox they been warning everbody about. Even dead, there's no tellin' what kind of contagion that wee thing might reek. It was covered with pust-holes, flies, the whole mess. Just rotting and dead when it was born. What else could I possibly do? I doused it with kerosene. Burnt it up. What else could I do?"

Lovell left the rail. He knelt before her. His hand cupped her chins.

"Yer smart as a whip, honey. You did just the right thing."

Both her hands came up fast, too fast, and clutched his.

"Mebbe I shoulda used *lime*. I coulda got some lime from Willy's store and covered the thing with that. It was such ugly sickness, Lovell. I keep suf-ferin' dreams of torment!"

Tough. He wanted to be tough. But nobody was tougher than a burnt baby or the whims of disease. He was afraid as she was. Fear put them silent. For several long minutes it gripped them, Lovell allow-ing her to clutch him while she wept feebly, eyes squeezed. When he spake, his feeling was genteel.

"Floy," he soothed, tearing from the clutch, "you have to go now."

A giant sob racked the porch swing. She yelped

out, "I get scary. Can't you come on back to the boudoir, pet me, gimme deep nookie?"

Lovell stood suddenly, swept back his silvering locks. "Nope. That can't happen."

"Buy me perty-perties…"

Just as abruptly, revelation struck him. He finally woke up without a pill. Lovell told her to wait then disappeared into the house. She waited.

A sunny scrim dropped over Floy and her sorrowful gaze. She glided the swing. Dawn brushed across flowertops in the garden, slicing through the arbor, gleaming off a belfry on a small belvedere for shade-sitting at the bottom of the yard. Ducks. Ducks went quack-quack nearby. What was this strange place, this big, spookhouse, this maze of trees and vine? Where was she? How had she gotten here? Her mind was going south. Floy sensed as much and felt more afraid.

Then, after a year and a half, Lovell was back on this strange porch. Returning to her. Returning from inside with his guitar. The devil's beard was gone. Wasn't that nice? Floy had never fancied his beard.

"Yer beard's gone—"

Lovell untied his rhinestone-braid guitar strap from the peg head, deftly unhooked the button end.

"—you lookin nice."

Setting his electric axe aside, he lay the strap across Floy's lap, flipping it over to the leather back-

side. His fingers found the hidden seam and the zip-
per within. Unzipping the strap, he exposed a secret
lining. It was flush with cash.

Floy's brow   creased   when   she   saw   the
folded money.

"Honey," he said, " you never knew, cause I
couldn't afford to tell you. But I had a feller make
this gitfiddle strap years ago, down in Chattanoo-
ger. He made and sold money belts so I figgered
he could sew me a rhinestone money strap just as
good. There's almost a solid grand in hyere. Nine
hunert dollars at least. I saved it. Kept a few bills
from you ever week."

Floy shut-up, dried-up, looking from the inner
green fold of legal tender, greenbacks—then back to
Lovell. He was fitting a pair of old tan bed slippers
on her feet. They were tight.

"This is all I kin give you, Floy," he was telling
her, "these shoes and this blanket to cover you proper, till you kin get home. These ain't walking shoes,
the dude who wore em took a even snugger fit in
his wingtips. You'd never fit into those. These'll jist
have to do. Here, keep this blanket around you,
there you go, no need fer everybody to see your bo-
soms, is there?"

Lovell got her on her feet then walked Floy down
the steps toward the road. She stumbled, hugging
her blanket and guitar strap beneath her chins. He
made her hold the blanket tight. He told her the

blanket was important, told her to keep her business out of the street.

"You take that boodle money," he advised, "don't tell nobody about it. Tuck it away somewhere only *you* know about. Don't fergit where you tuck it. I see things have changed fer you, Floy. But yer gonna have to do some more changing still. Just spend a little of that green at a time. Only when you really need it."

She stopped, turned and looked bluntly at him. It occurred to her that Lovell wasn't coming along. How could that be?

"...You gotta learn to live differnt than you ever have, hon," he was saying, "we all do. You save this cash. You git back on your feet. But you cain't never come back here. I cain't help you no more." He hated himself for saying it, but he said it. "Fergive me."

Lovell thought she might boo-hoo again, when he asked that.

But she did not. Instead, Floy made cheerful, after a fashion—hooking stiff strands behind each ear, struggling for a brave face. Her snaggle-toothed words finally came:

"Don't be thinkin you wasn't anointed. You and that guitar you love. You was the jack o'spades."

Yes, he thought. But, no.

"You ain't got to be anointed," he said, "to know whether love rubs right or wrong."

That's all he did say.

"Thank you, doll."

"No problem."

"You bought me pertier perties than any man I ever knew."

"Gives me a strong feelin', knowin' that."

Fionuala was sipping her special blend of chicory and cocoa when he found her in the Florida room. From the shade of the rubber tree her swollen eyes smiled. Kissing her lips lightly, he hummed a few bluesy notes. Sinking into his chair, buttoning his vest, he hummed a few more.

"You had company?" Fina whispered ever so gently.

"Mmmm-hmmm."

"You could have invited them in for Mad Rabbit Stew. But, only if you wanted to."

He took up the guitar. Without voltage, Lovell chorded a slow-thumping blues. He sang, barely.

Baby, it's a crime
   you ain't never been kissed,
      Whaaaaaaay-yell,
         We all lose our heads
            on the Axman's shift—

His riff soured, he stopped, then—*TWAAAAAANG*— his left hand shot down the D-string. Gleaming fire and bedevilment, Lovell gave her the eye.

"What you want fer breakfast, Fionuala Brynn?" he asked, smacking his chops.

Fionuala leaned forth, warbled her own flat, airy melody: "Another *aelspin* song, sir. Yes, another song. Oooh. yes, then another..."

His discharged axe tossed off a couple of spry boogies before she told him her secret. That little room with nursery carol wallpaper would soon be a nursery once again. Ten long seconds later he made a proposal. When Wednesday came her lawyer was introduced to Sir Lovell Starling of the Chesapeake Starlings.

They married that weekend down in Roanoke, swearing vows before a justice the lawyer knew well. They never exchanged rings. Neither Fionuala or Lovell saw the need. Two hours later they visited the doctor, a doctor Fina and the lawyer knew well, and the doc gave them both his blessing.

Winter crept in as she outgrew her dresses. November found him signing away the mineral rights to his Alabama parcel. The two were seen together more and more, sometimes even strolling through Ewe Springs and Cayuga Ridge. The expectant bird in her swathing and dark shades, cooing an arcane tongue to her swarthy gitpicker. It was quite a shock. They kept mostly to themselves in that twelve-gabled manor house up Six Bucket Run, especially once the snows reached full bluster. She could not travel easily by then, so they waited for Spring's gift. He carried good fuses in his pocket at all times. In the icicled evenings, tuning up before the woodfire, he thought he might get around to asking how her family made all of this loot. Maybe he should inquire about her mother someday. These were just chords to ponder. Shortly, he began crooning left-handed boogaloos to that woodfire, boogaloos that turned into lullabies. She rocked easily. She looked out and sang along.

Other books by Randy Thornhorn:

THE KESTREL WATERS
A Tale Of Love And Devil
(sequel to *Wicked Temper*)

WICKED TEMPER
A Riddle Top Novel

HOWLS OF A HELLHOUND ELECTRIC
Riddle Top Magpies & Bobnot Boogies

Visit Randy Thornhorn online at

www.thornhorn.com

www.ingramcontent.com/pod-product-compliance
Lightning Source LLC
Chambersburg PA
CBHW020317150626
46552CB00022B/2909

* 9 7 8 0 9 9 1 6 4 9 6 6 2 *